British Library Cataloguing in Publication Data
Willis, Jeanne
  Dr. Xargle's book of earthlets.
  1. Babies
  I. Title   II. Ross, Tony, *1938-*
  305.2'32
  ISBN 0-86264-213-2

Text © 1988 by Jeanne Willis. Illustrations © 1988 by Tony Ross. First
published in Great Britain in 1988 by Andersen Press Ltd., 62–65 Chandos
Place, London WC2. Published in Australia by Century Hutchinson Australia
Pty. Ltd., 16–22 Church Street, Hawthorn, Victoria 3122. All rights reserved.
Colour separated in Switzerland by Photolitho AG Offsetreproduktionen,
Gossau, Zürich. Printed in Great Britain by W. S. Cowell Ltd., Ipswich.

DR XARGLE'S
BOOK OF
EARTHLETS

Translated into Human by Jeanne Willis
Pictures by Tony Ross

Andersen Press · London
Hutchinson · Australia

Good morning, class.

Today we are going to learn about Earthlets.

They come in four colours. Pink, brown, black or yellow ... but not green.

They have one head and only two eyes, two short tentacles with pheelers on the end and two long tentacles called leggies.

They have square claws which they use to frighten off
wild beasts known as Tibbles and Marmaduke.

Earthlets grow fur on their heads but not enough to keep them warm.

They must be wrapped in the hairdo of a sheep.

Very old Earthlings (or "Grannies") unravel the sheep and with two pointed sticks they make Earthlet wrappers in blue and white and pink.

Earthlets have no fangs at birth.
For many days they drink only milk through a hole in their face.

When they have finished the milk they must be patted and squeezed to stop them exploding.

When they grow a fang, the parent Earthling takes the egg of a hen and mangles it with a prong.

Then she puts the eggmangle on a small spade and
tips it into the Earthlet's mouth, nose and ears.

To stop them leaking, Earthlets must be pulled up by the back tentacles and folded in half.
Then they must be wrapped quickly in a fluffy triangle or sealed with paper and glue.

During the day, Earthlets collect the hairs of Tibbles and Marmaduke, mud, eggmangle and banana.

They are then placed in plastic capsules with warm water and a yellow floating bird.

After soaking, Earthlets must be dried carefully to
stop them shrinking.
Then they are sprinkled with dust to stop them
sticking to things.

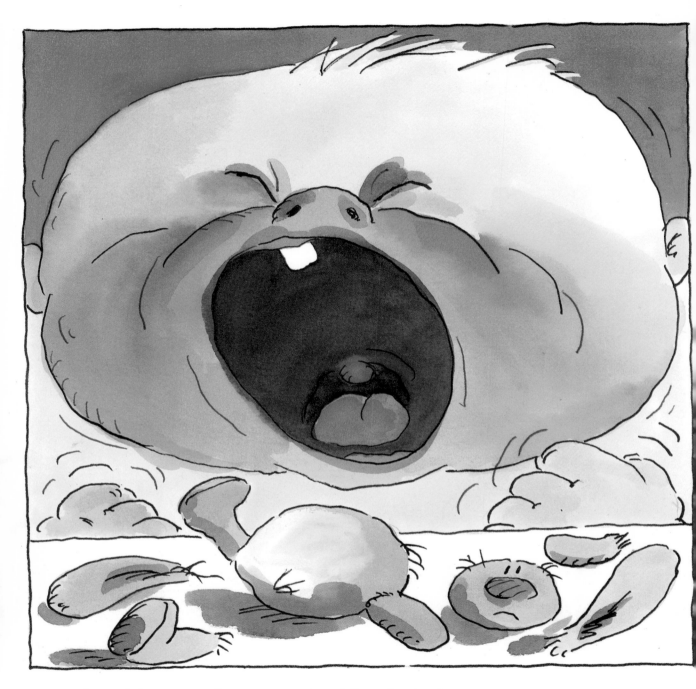

Earthlets can be recognised by their fierce cry,
"WAAAAAAA!"

To stop them doing this, the Earthling daddy picks them up and flings them into the atmosphere.

Then he tries to catch them.

If they still cry, the Earthling mummy pulls their pheelers one by one and says "This little piggy went to market" until the Earthlet makes a "hee hee" noise.

If they still cry, they are sent to a place called
beddybyes.

This is a swinging box with a soft lining in which
there lives a small bear called Teddy.

That is the end of today's lesson.

If you are all very good and quiet we are going to put
our disguises on and visit planet Earth to see some
real Earthlets.

The spaceship leaves in five minutes.